Designed by Cathy L. Colbert

Text by Debbie Weissmann

"Pooh's Sweet Dreams Song" by Amy Edgar, from

Winnie the Pooh's Bedtime Hummables, copyright © 2000 by Disney Enterprises, Inc.

For more Disney Press fun, visit www.disneybooks.com

For information address Disney Press, 114 Fifth Avenue, New York, New York 10011-5690.

Printed in the United States of America.

Based on the Pooh Stories by A. A. Milne

(Copyright The Pooh Properties Trust)

FIRST EDITION

1 3 5 7 9 10 8 6 4 2

Library of Congress Catalog Card Number on file

ISBN 0-7868-3289-4

Disney's
Winnie the Pooh
and
YOU

Written by _____
(your name here)

Drawings by _____
(your name here)

Disney PRESS

New York

"Hoo-hoo-hoo-hallooo!"

Winnie the Pooh and his friends want to create a book about a very important person: you! And they need your help.

So please fill in the blanks, draw pictures in the boxes, and paste in some photographs. When you have finished, you will have a new book all about Winnie the Pooh and you!

All About Me

My name is

I am

_____ feet _____ inches tall.

When I stand
on the scale,
I weigh _____ pounds.

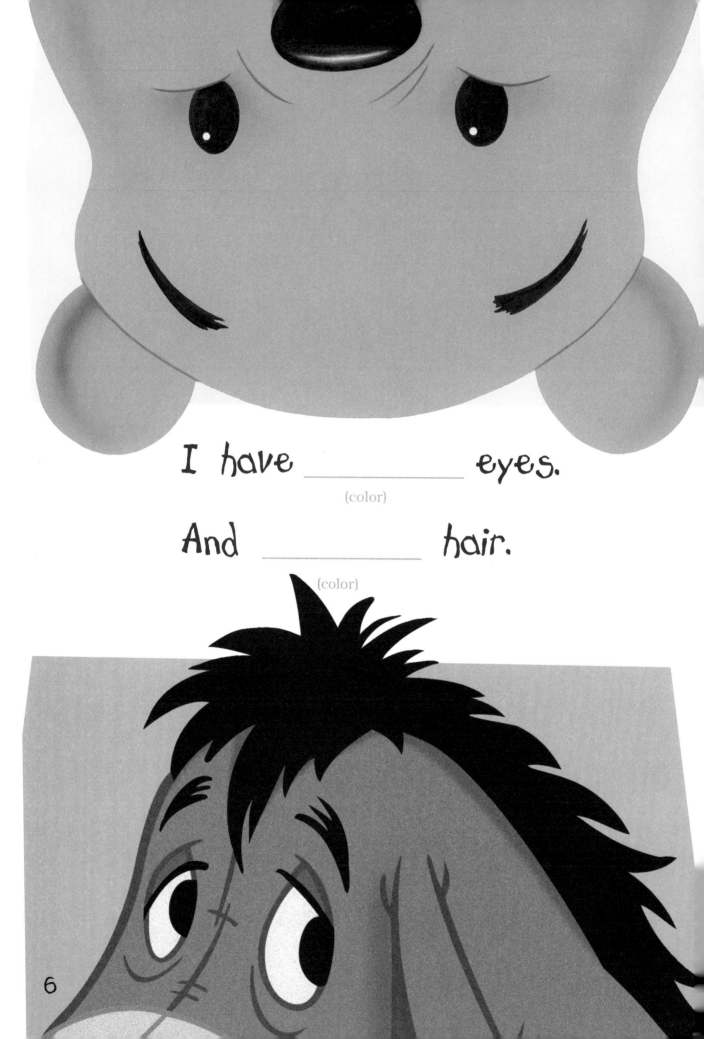

I have _____ eyes.
(color)

And _____ hair.
(color)

6

This is a photograph of me.

(Paste 5 x 7 photo here.)

7

When I stretch my arms out as far as I can, I can stretch _____ inches.

I usually use
my right / my left / either hand
(Circle one.)
8   when I write.

My hand is this big.

(Trace the outline of your hand.)

When I take just one step,
I step _____ inches.

When I jump,
I can jump
_____ inches.

My shoes are size _____.

And, my foot is this big.

(Trace the outline of your foot.)

Here are some things I can do.

(Check the box next to every activity you can do.)

I can bounce.

I can touch my toes.

I can read a book.

I can climb a tree.

I can spin around
five times in a row
without falling down.

I can do these things, too:

_____

_____

My Family and Friends

Here are the names of the people in my family.

Here is a picture of me and _____.

(Paste photo here.)

Here is a picture of me
and my family:

Other important members of my family are:

(Here is a good place to name grandparents, uncles, aunts, cousins.)

_____

- -

_____

- -

_____

- -

_____

Here are pictures of them:

I have / do not have **a pet.**
(Circle one.)

Here is a picture of my pet /
the pet I'd most like to have:
(Circle one.)

Here are some pictures
of the animals that I like
from magazines and newspapers.

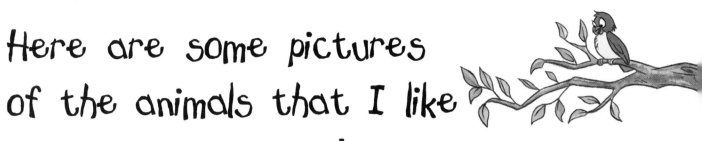

(Cut them out and paste here.)

My very best friend is named

_____ .

The very best thing about my very best
friend is _____ .

Together, we love to _____

_____ .

18

Here is a little poem about me and my very best friend.

With _____ , my friend,
    (friend's name)

   I love to play.

We _____ , _____ , and
   (action word)   (action word)

_____ every day.
(action word)

We bounce like Tigger

   When he's playing with Roo.

We _____ like Rabbit
      (action word)

   Who has so much to do.

We swim like Eeyore

   In the river so blue.

And sing silly hums

   Just like Winnie the Pooh.

My Home

Owl lives way up high in a chestnut tree.
When he is home, which he often is,
he sits in his rocking chair, and rocks
back and forth, back and forth.

My address is:

I have my own special place in my home.
It is MY ROOM.

I share my room with _____.

I like my room because _____.

I have pictures of _____
hanging on the wall.

This is a map of my home.

(Make a map of all the rooms in your home
and be sure to show where your room is.)

My room is in my home and my home is in my neighborhood. There are lots of other things in my neighborhood, too. There is my school, the grocery store, the park I play in, and my very best friend's house.

The best place to play in my neighborhood is _____.

The best pets in my neighborhood are _____

This is a map of my neighborhood:

And this is a map of
Winnie the Pooh's neighborhood.

I can find Pooh's House, Rabbit's Carrot Patch, Eeyore's
Gloomy Place, and the bridge for tossing Pooh Sticks.

(Put a circle around each one you find. Circle where you would live in the Hundred-Acre Wood.)

There are lots of special people in my neighborhood. Some of them have signed my book.

Mail Carrier

Firefighter

Police Officer

Grocer

Teacher

Someone Who Has a Cat

Someone Who Has a Dog

Someone Who Likes Winnie the Pooh

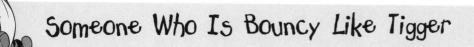

Someone Who Is Bouncy Like Tigger

Sometimes I think about what I will do when I grow up.
I will be a _____.

This is a picture of me doing my job when I am a grown-up.

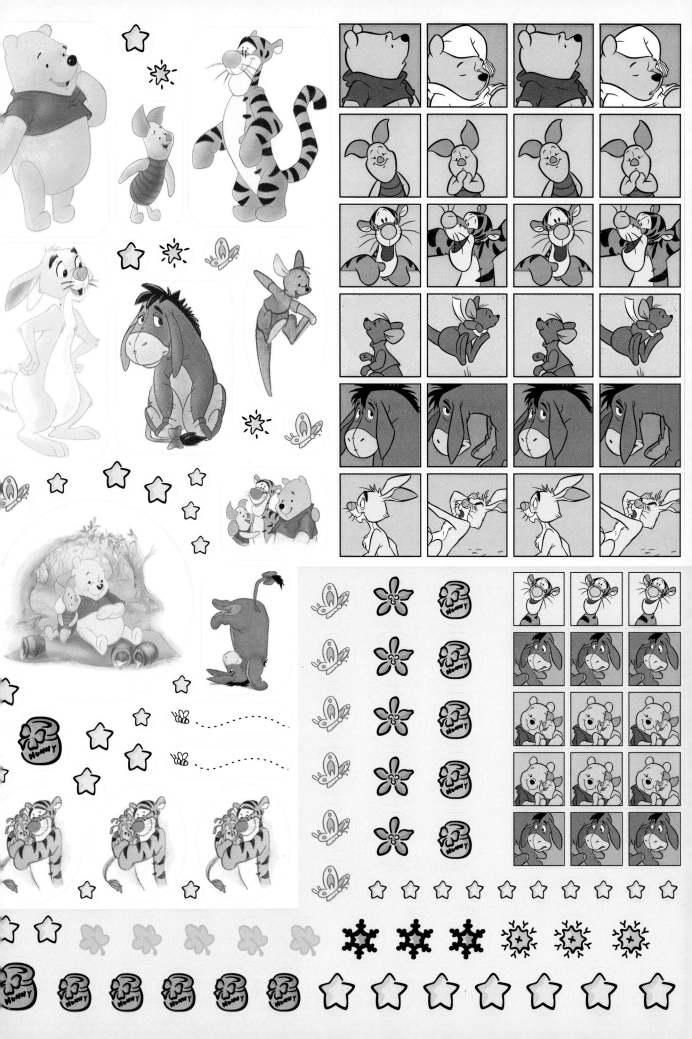

These are some interesting things that are happening in

My Neighborhood.

(Paste headlines or articles from your local or school newspaper here.)

My School

I have reached that certain age when I have begun to go to school.

The name of my school is _____

_____ .

It takes ___ minutes to get to school.

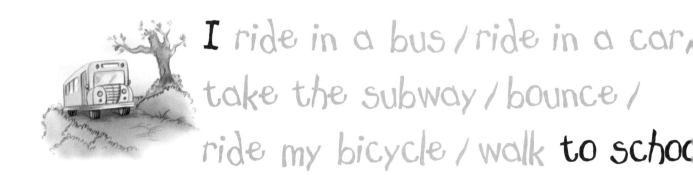

I ride in a bus / ride in a car / take the subway / bounce / ride my bicycle / walk to school

(Circle one.)

I am in the _____ grade.

My teacher's name is

_____ .

My favorite subject is

_____ .

The best field trip ever was to

_____ .

Here is some artwork that I made at school.

I had lots of / some / little / no help with it.

(Circle one.)

My Birthday and Other Favorite Days

I was born on _____ .
(date)

I was born at _____ .
(time)

I weighed this much when I was born:
_____ pounds, _____ ounces.

That is about as much as (Circle one.)

One haycorn 🌰   One honeypot 🍯

This is where I was born: _____

_____ .

These are the names of some people who saw me right after I was born:

_____

_____

This is what I looked like when I was very small:

(Paste photograph here.)

I looked most like
(Circle one.)

I acted most like
(Circle one.)

Today I am _____ years old.
On my next birthday I will be
_____ years old.

I will / will not blow out all
(Circle one.)
the candles on my cake in one breath.

On birthdays my family loves to

_____ .

For my last birthday,
the best toy I got was

_____ .

If I made up my own toy,
this is what it would look like:

For my next birthday I hope
I get a _____ .

My favorite holiday is

_____

because _____

_____ .

This holiday happens in

_____ .

(month)

Here is a picture of me celebrating my favorite holiday.

(Draw or paste a picture here.)

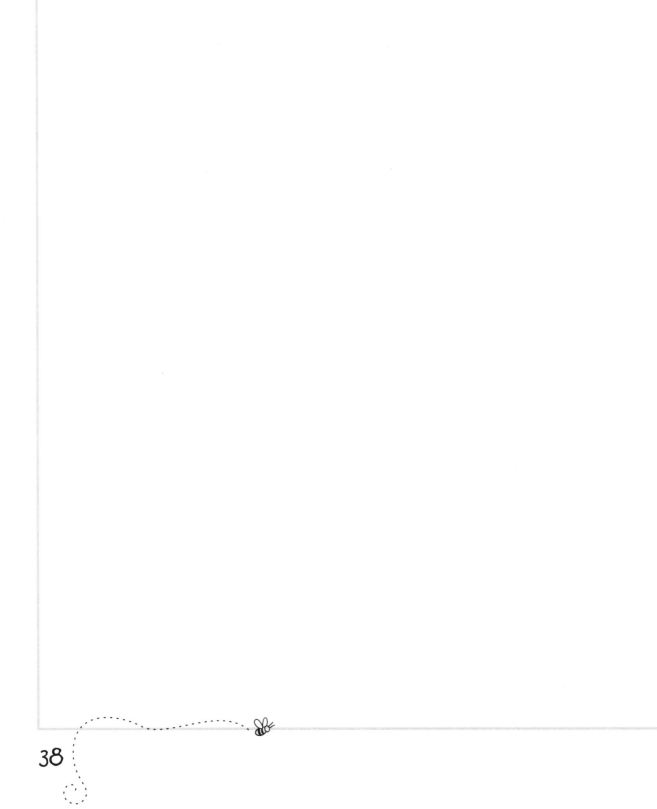

38

Sometimes I go on vacation!
My favorite vacation was

_____ .

The part of the trip that was the
most fun was _____

_____ .

I went with _____ .

Paste photos or postcards here.

WISH YOU
WERE HERE!

If I could go on vacation anywhere at all, I would go to _____.

I would bring these people: _____

_____

I would need to pack these things:

_____

_____

This is a drawing of me on my perfect vacation:

More About Me

I have told you about the outside
of me. There is also an inside of me.
The inside of me is how I feel and
what I think about when I think
about things.

My Feelings

When I am happy, there are some things I do to show it. I have circled all the ones that I do:

I smile.

I bounce.

I do a flip.

I sing.

I laugh.

I clap my hands.

I dance around.

I _____ .
(Fill in something you do when you are happy.)

Sometimes I am sad.
When I am sad, I _____

_____

(Fill in what you do to feel better, like hugging a special blanket.)

and I feel less sad.

"Good morning!" called Pooh.
"Are you sure?" Eeyore looked at the sky.
"Would you call that blue, Pooh? Or gray?
At least it's not raining," he added. "Yet."

My favorite feeling is
(Check one.)

Happy

Excited

Silly

Other: _____

I usually
feel this
way when

_____

Here is a picture of me when I'm feeling my favorite feeling.

(Draw or paste a picture here.)

45

More Favorites

My favorite friend from the
Hundred-Acre Wood is _____

because _____ .

I am most like _____
(Pick one of the friends.)

because _____ .

My favorite color is _____ .

(Find a color pen or crayon to write the name of your favorite color here.)

(You can draw a picture using your favorite color, too.)

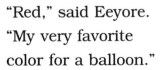

"Red," said Eeyore.
"My very favorite
color for a balloon."

My favorite season of the year is
(Circle one.)

Winter

Spring

Summer

Fall

48

Here is a picture of what my favorite season looks like when I am outside, in the middle of it.

Pooh's favorite food is honey.

My favorite food is _____ .

I eat it with

a knife/a fork/a spoon/my fingers.
(Circle one.)

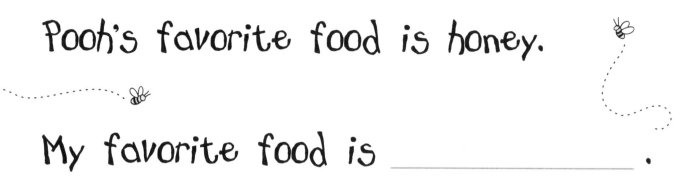

Now Pooh was not
the sort to give up easily.
When he put his mind to
honey, he stuck to it.

50

I eat as much as Piglet.

True / False
(Circle one.)

I eat as much
as Tigger.

True / False
(Circle one.)

I eat as much as
Winnie the Pooh.

True / False
(Circle one.)

(Oh my!)

The one food that I really don't like is _____ .

Someone who really likes this food is _____ .

They can eat a pinch / a plate,
(Circle one.)
a barrel of this food

Yuck! Tiggers don't like honey!
That icky, sticky stuff is only fit
for heffalumps and woozles!

My favorite thing to
wear is _____ .

Here is a picture of
me wearing my favorite
thing to wear.

Each morning, Pooh
would change out of
his sleeping pajamas
into his day clothes,
which turned out
to be not very many
clothes at all.

These are all of my favorite games to play:

Winnie the Pooh, Piglet, Rabbit, Roo, and Tigger all lined up
on one side of the bridge and dropped their sticks into the
river. When the sticks were no longer in sight, they turned to
the other side of the bridge to watch whose stick would come
out first. And that was how they played the game, Pooh Sticks,
named after Pooh because he invented it.

Of all the songs I know, and I know of many songs to sing, my favorite song is

_____
(title)

And some of the words go like this:

_____

_____

_____

_____

_____

I have a favorite place where I go to think, and it is _____ .
Here is a thought I had today while I was in my favorite thinking place.

(Write a thought or a hum here.)

Winnie the Pooh had a Thoughtful Spot where he would go when he had a thought to think. And, as he sat in his Thoughtful Spot he would tap himself on the head and say, "Think, Think, Think."

My favorite book is

It was written by

I have read it one / two / three / four /
(Circle one.)
more than four times.

The best part is when

My favorite spot
to read books is

58

If I wrote my own book (besides this one!), it would be all about

_____ .

This is what the cover would look like:

How I Go to Sleep

I have one last thing to tell about me.

I sleep in a
large / small / bunk bed.
(Circle one.)

I like the light off / dim / on
(Circle one.)
when I fall asleep.

And just before I fall
asleep, I _____

_____

_____

(What do you do before you fall asleep?
Do you say prayers, kiss mom or dad,
read by yourself?)

60

Pooh's Sweet Dreams Song

I'm tucked in bed all snuggledy tight,
Where things are always cuddledy right.
Snoozle-tea-pie, snoozle-tea-pie.

Sweet dreams will come to me tonight,
And soon will come the morning light.
Snoozle-tea-pie, snoozle-tea-pie.

Let's End with the End

And now I come to the end of my book.
I must get on to the other sorts of things
that I like to do, such as those things I
have written about in this book.

I finished this book on _____,
                                                    (day of week)

_____ _____, _____.
        (month)   (date)   (year)

TTFN

(Ta-Ta For Now)